THE
CHOCOLATE WOLF

Barbara Cohen

illustrated by David Ray

Philomel Books • New York

Text copyright © 1996 by The Estate of Barbara Cohen
Illustrations copyright © 1996 by David Ray
All rights reserved. This book, or parts thereof, may not be reproduced in any form
without permission in writing from the publisher. Philomel Books, a division of
The Putnam & Grosset Group, 200 Madison Avenue, New York, NY 10016.
Philomel Books, Reg. U.S. Pat. & Tm. Off. Published simultaneously in Canada.
Printed in Singapore. Book design by Gunta Alexander. The text is set in Administer.

Library of Congress Cataloging-in-Publication Data
Cohen, Barbara.   The chocolate wolf / by Barbara Cohen; illustrated by David Ray
p.   cm.   Summary: A chocolate wolf escapes from a candy store and finds himself
in a desperate situation with a family of hungry rats.
[1. Candy–Fiction.   Wolves–Fiction.   3. Rats–Fiction.] I. Ray, David, ill.   II. Title.
PZ7.C6595Cg 1996 [E]–dc20 91-46434 CIP AC ISBN 0-399-21961-7

10 9 8 7 6 5 4 3 2 1 First Impression

For Levi, Jacob, Yasmin, Catriona,
Nadav, Gonen, and Mahri—B.C.

With Love for Melissa and Alysa—D.R.

The Candy Man made animals out of marzipan, peppermint, and chocolate. His assistant, Sylvester, helped him. Mostly they produced cats, dogs, rabbits, and ducks. Now and then they

created an elephant, a zebra, a wildebeest, or a rhinoceros.
The Candy Man charged more for exotic animals.

One day while working in chocolate, he made a mistake. The animal's nose was too long, its ears were too long, its tail was too long. "That's the oddest dog I've ever seen," said Sylvester.

"There's definitely something wrong with him," the Candy Man agreed.

"It isn't a dog at all," Sylvester said.

"Then what is it?"

Sylvester stared at the animal for a long time. "It's a wolf," he announced at last.

"Good," said the Candy Man. "A wolf is exotic. I can get more for a wolf."

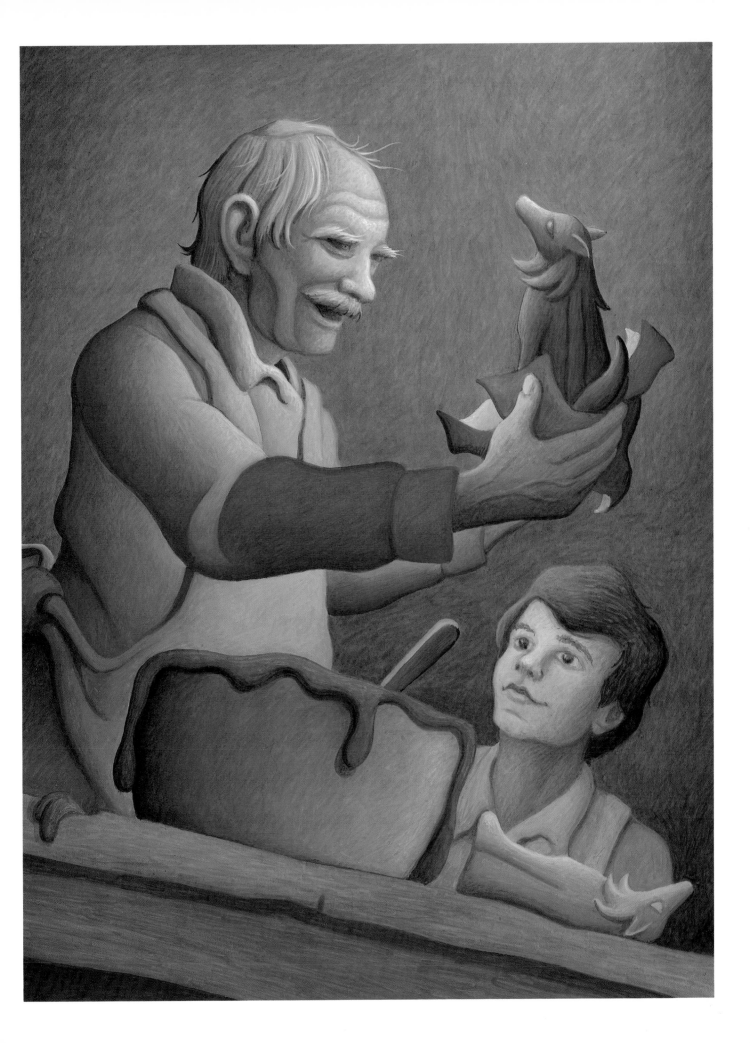

But he couldn't. Twin girls came in. They spent their birth-day money on two lambs and a platypus. They didn't buy the Chocolate Wolf.

A young couple came in. They chose an armadillo for their baby. They didn't buy the Chocolate Wolf.

A woman filled a huge shopping bag to the top with candy animals. But although she bought almost everything else in the store, she didn't buy the Chocolate Wolf. "I don't like wolves," she said. "They eat people."

The Candy Man lowered the price on the Chocolate Wolf. It didn't help. Week after week the Chocolate Wolf sat in the glass case. No one wanted him. "What's the matter with me?" he cried. "Why doesn't anyone buy me?"

The shop was closed. The Candy Man had gone home. Sylvester was alone, polishing the cases. "Don't feel too bad about it," he told the Chocolate Wolf. "At least you're not getting eaten."

"Eaten?" exclaimed the Chocolate Wolf. "Is that what happens to the animals in this place?"

"Yes," Sylvester replied. "Eventually."

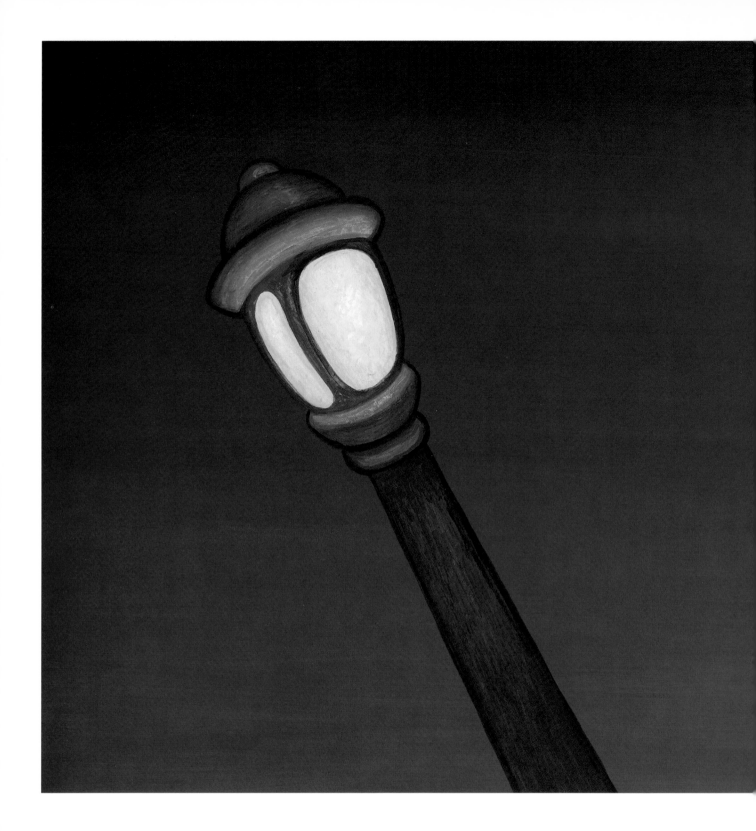

In the dim chill of the silent shop, the Chocolate Wolf shivered.

Sylvester left the glass case open just a crack. He left the window open just a crack. And then he went home.

The Chocolate Wolf squeezed through the crack in the

glass case. He squeezed through the crack in the window.
He jumped from the sill to the sidewalk.

He looked around. The street was dark and quiet. No
moon, no stars. The only light came from the streetlamp.

A man and a woman came laughing and singing down the street. "Oh, look, Bert!" the woman cried. "A piece of chocolate. I love chocolate." She picked up the wolf and opened her mouth wide.

Bert grabbed her wrist. "Don't be childish, Marjorie. You can't eat things off the sidewalk. They're full of germs."

Regretfully, Marjorie dropped the Chocolate Wolf. A piece of his tail broke off. He scampered out of the way and pressed himself against the cement wall of the nearest building.

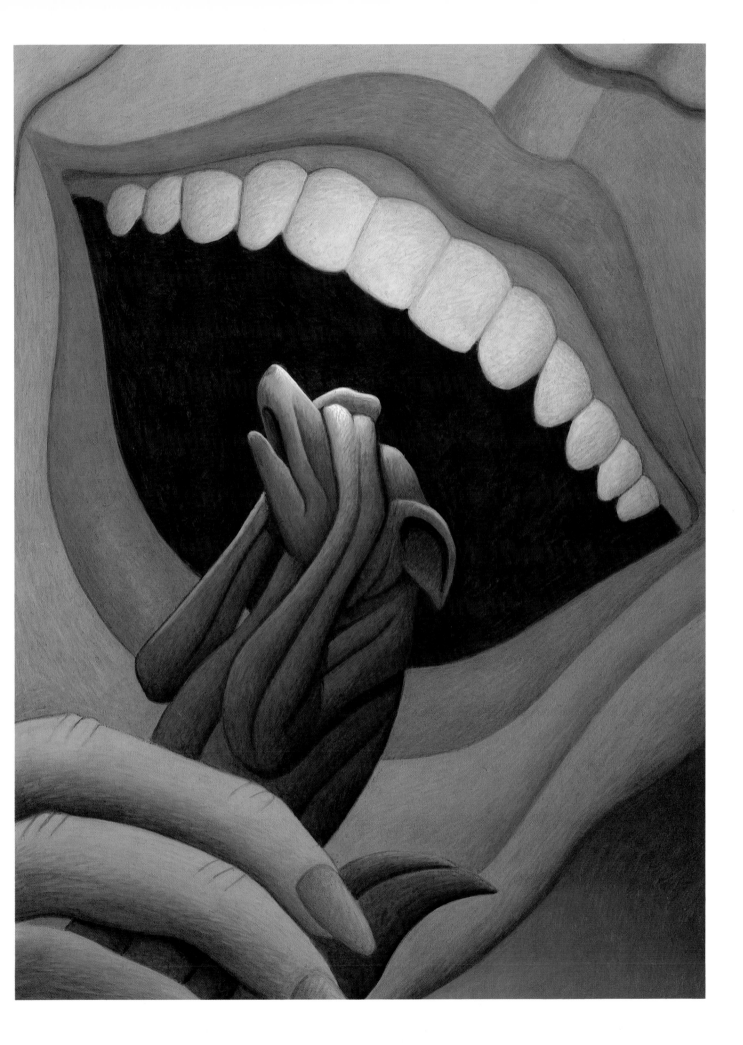

A wave of weariness overcame him. He felt as if his legs would no longer hold him. He stared at his front paws. They seemed to be growing soft and mushy. They were melting!

Just in time, the Chocolate Wolf realized he was standing next to a heating vent. He ran across the sidewalk, jumped off the curb, and landed in the gutter.

For a moment, he rested comfortably between a crumpled cigar wrapper and a half-eaten loaf of bread. But no sooner had he caught his breath, when he noticed two lights rolling toward him. A large wagon lumbered down the street. As it moved, a huge brush attached to it swept up and seemed to swallow all the litter in its way.

The Chocolate Wolf leaped back onto the sidewalk. No place was safe, no place.

A rat and his wife were out for their nightly prowl. Their seven skinny rat children walked behind them in a row.

The Chocolate Wolf was so glad to see other creatures more or less his own size that he hurried toward them. "Why is it so dark out here?" he asked.

"The moon and stars are covered with clouds," said Mr. Rat.

"It's going to rain," said Mrs. Rat.

"Rain!" cried the Chocolate Wolf. He remembered the heating vent. "I might melt in the rain."

The rat children sniffed his toes, his tail, and his whiskers.

Mrs. Rat smiled graciously, showing all her rat teeth. "Come home with us. We live under a porch."

The largest rat child nipped at the Chocolate Wolf's heel.

The Chocolate Wolf jumped. "Stop that, Edgar!" Mr. Rat
shouted. "Wait until we get home."

"Don't mind Edgar," Mrs. Rat said, still smiling her toothy
smile. "He's high-spirited." She sent him to the end of the line.
"Behave yourself," she scolded, "or you won't get anything."

The Chocolate Wolf walked home between Mr. and Mrs. Rat. Beneath the porch, the rat family possessed every comfort. "Your place is lovely," the wolf said.

"Thank you," said Mrs. Rat as she and her husband settled themselves on a pile of rags and straw. "Join us, please."

"Is it time now?" Edgar asked.

"No," said Mrs. Rat. "First poke your nose out and make sure they haven't let that awful dog out into the yard."

Edgar peered through the entry hole. "All clear," he said. He sat down next to his father. "Is it time now?"

"No," said Mr. Rat. "Now we listen to the story."

The Chocolate Wolf heard a steady *creak, creak* above his head. "What's that?" he asked.

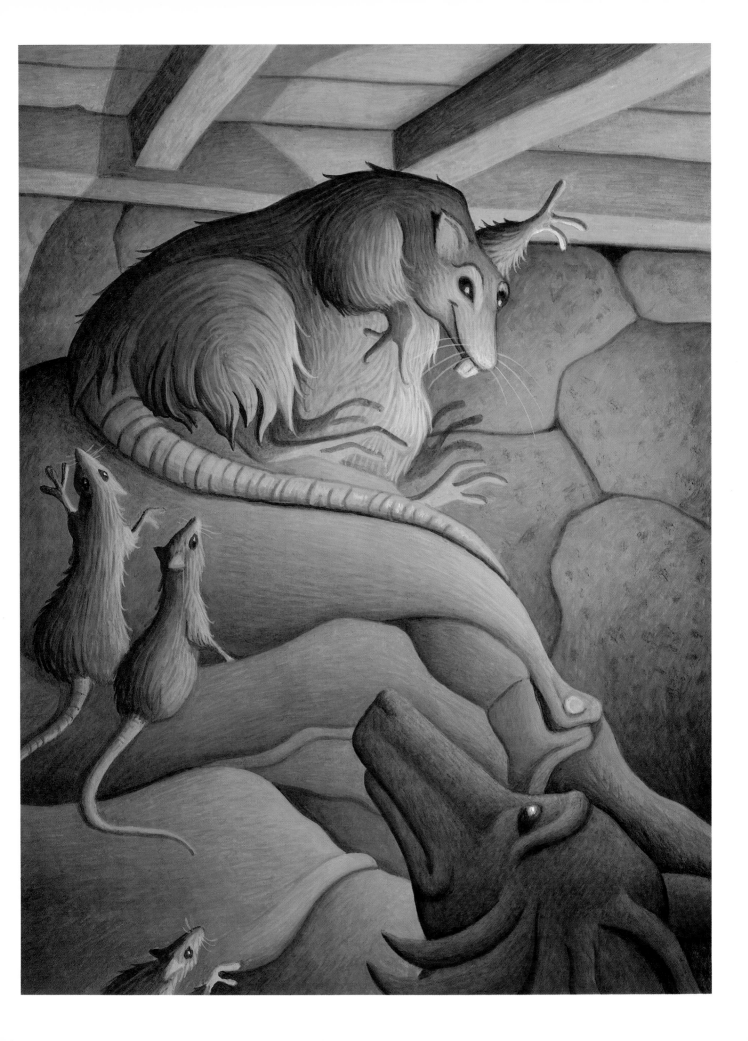

"The mother," Mr. Rat explained. "Or the father. One of them sits in a rocking chair on the porch every night with their boy and tells him a story. We always listen."

That night it was the mother who held the boy on her lap. "Well, Levi," the Chocolate Wolf heard the mother say,

"what will it be tonight?"

"Three Billy Goats Gruff," said Levi.

The mother told a story about three goats outwitting a mean troll who wanted to eat them up. The rats applauded at the end. So did the Chocolate Wolf.

"Now it's time for bed," the mother said.

"Another story, please," Levi begged.

"Well, just one more," said his mother. "Which will it be?"

"The Three Little Pigs and the Big Bad Wolf," said Levi.

"I wonder if it's so smart to tell stories about wolves right before you go to sleep," his mother replied. But she told the story anyway. It was about three pigs outwitting a mean wolf who wanted to eat them up. Again, the rats applauded. "I didn't like that one so much," the Chocolate Wolf commented.

But no one heard him. "It's time for dinner," Mrs. Rat announced.

The young rats leaped to their feet and rushed toward the Chocolate Wolf, Edgar in the lead. The Chocolate Wolf realized *he* was the dinner. He headed for the entry hole, but Mr. Rat stood in front of it, barring the way.

This is it, thought the Chocolate Wolf. His whole life flashed before him.

Suddenly, Mr. Rat fell down. A large paw appeared behind him, and the raucous sound of barking filled the air.

"That awful dog is here again!" cried Mrs. Rat. "Run, children, run!"

In a flash, all the rats had disappeared. The dog pulled his paw out of the hole, stuck his nose in, and sniffed. Then he pulled his nose out again. The Chocolate Wolf ran out of the rats' house as fast as his legs would carry him.

The dog barked, sprang at the Chocolate Wolf, and landed

on his belly, surrounding the wolf with his two front legs. His long, slurpy tongue licked a chocolate paw.

This is it, thought the Chocolate Wolf. Once again, his whole life flashed before him.

Levi ran down the porch steps. "Dog! What have you got there!"

The dog looked up at the boy. Slowly he rose to his feet
and backed away.

Levi knelt down on the ground. "A wolf!" he exclaimed. "Are
you going to eat me up, Wolf?"

"No," said the wolf. "Are you going to eat me up, Boy?"

"No," said the boy.

He carried the Chocolate Wolf up to his room and put him
on top of his dresser, where no one could get him.

And there they lived happily together for a long, long time.